D1711840

GUARDIAN
of the STONES

NAT AND MATEO DISCOVER THE
TWO FORCES OF THE MAGIC STONES

WRITTEN & ILLUSTRATED BY
MARTIN WELLING

outskirtspress

DENVER, COLORADO

To Hailee, Nathan and Kaitlyn

Outskirts Press, Inc.
http://www.outskirtspress.com

ISBN: 978-1-4327-7692-3

Outskirts Press and the "OP" logo are trademarks belonging to Outskirts Press, Inc.

PRINTED IN THE UNITED STATES OF AMERICA

$\mathcal{N}$at felt lucky to live so close to what he considered the most stirring and beautiful place in the world. His house sat off to one side of a lot wider than it was deep. Mature pine trees, bent and leaning toward the sea, were tall enough to put his white wood-planked house in total shade during the morning hours. Struggling for lack of sunlight, uneven patches of grass sprinkled the surface of the front yard. In poorly defined flowerbeds up against the house, oversized Birds of Paradise created a pleasant tropical look with an abundance of orange and yellow spiked blossoms. The twenty-foot-high bluff in back, capped by a freshly painted picket fence, conspicuously marked the end of their property and afforded them an almost magical view of the ocean.

Nat's day began like many others before it. Without much thought, he pulled on the same surf shorts he had worn the day before, added a fresh t-shirt, washed his hands and face, and brushed his teeth. Breakfast consisted of warm oatmeal – cold milk puddled on the surface, darkened here and there with brown sugar – a hard-boiled egg, and two pieces of well-done bacon. A half glass each of chocolate milk and orange juice stood like sentinels on both sides of his relic, superhero-patterned bowl. In addition to making him breakfast, his mother had prepared him a snack and left it in a bag on the kitchen table.

Nat could see from the discarded plates in the sink that his father had already left for work. Mother was outside, busily tending to her small garden along the side of the house. The vegetable plants growing in the raised garden box were beginning to fade, while newly sown flowers were just breaking the surface of the dark, wet soil. Mother loved the tasks associated with planting, pruning, and encouraging her wistful plants. Only the damage caused by hungry squirrels ever prompted her to feel anything other than pure joy in her garden.

Finishing his last gulp of chocolate milk, Nat reached for his backpack, already weighted down with old gardening tools and several discarded plastic food containers with snap-on lids. He inserted his snack bag into his backpack, swung his arms through the straps, and headed out the back door. The air outside was already warming, and the overnight fog had retreated several hundred yards offshore.

Bounding down the back steps, he tossed a glance at his bikes – the new red one and last year's blue, smaller version, nested into each other up against the side of the house. Picturing himself driving the family car in a few years, Nat foresaw the new bike being his last. Walking quickly, Nat headed directly toward the back right corner of his shallow backyard. Within moments, he was at the crest of the bluff. An opening in the fence introduced the descending sun-bleached wooden stairs. From this vantage point, he could see that a large bundle of seaweed and an old car tire had washed ashore overnight. Dropping from one leg to the other in quick unison, he deftly maneuvered the stairs and climbed his way down the thirty or so steps to the sandy shore.

A quick inspection of the old tire and tangled seaweed reminded Nat of the time he had accompanied his father on an errand to put new tires on their van. As unusual as it was to have a car tire wash ashore, Nat knew that it probably hadn't come from a car at all. Many of the local fishing boats used old tires as docking pads, and this one must have worn free from its tethers on the side of a passing boat. Nat picked up the treadless tire and dragged it up against the large bed of blossoming ice plant growing at the base of the bluff. He would do his best later to hoist it up the stairs and ask his father to recycle it at the tire shop.

In deciding what direction he would hike, either up or down the beach, Nat thoughtfully weighed his options. Heading north up the shore would require navigating around a rocky outcropping that edged a narrow tide pool. In high surf, this obstacle ensured he would get wet, as tall wave sets tumbled onto the rocks and sprayed cold, salty, rejuvenating water over the shallow tide pool. Recognizing the retreating low tide, Nat confidently headed north and took his chances of getting a little wet.

Although a strong swimmer, Nat knew the strength of the rolling water along the waterfront had to be respected. He knew he had to be careful to avoid being washed off a perch or pulled off his feet into the retreating ebb of the breaking waves. Most of the time he avoided the surging water altogether by walking the shoreline in the dry sand above the reach of the breaking waves. The soft sand slowed his pace, but ensured his safety.

Nat pulled off his sneakers and tied the shoelaces around his waist like a belt – positioning one shoe in front, and the other in back under his backpack. He playfully strolled forward through the warming sand, enjoying the feeling under his feet. Every few minutes his gaze would drift out over the breaking waves and beyond. He remembered once being told, by his best friend Mateo, that the visible edge of the horizon was only three miles away – it looked much further.

Mateo lived close by – only two blocks north and one block inland from Nat's house. He lived with his mother in a tidy, well-kept home, with the best-manicured lawn and flowerbeds in their neighborhood. Mateo's bedroom, with its stylish furniture and large TV, made Nat a little envious. They both attended the same school and had been lucky to be in the same class three times over the years, including Mrs. Streicher's class last year. They both enjoyed the commotion of school and best liked their science studies and the competition associated with their intramural sports activities. Although too young to make a definitive career choice, they had a shared dream of becoming either marine biologists or professional athletes.

Mateo and Nat often hung out together, and had made their parents comfortable over the years with their decision-making and choices. Together they had a short but respectable run in a local Boy Scout program where they had earned a handful of awards that heightened their safety and good citizen awareness. They could be often mischievous and too adventurous, but never destructive or disrespectful. Mateo had spent the last few weeks visiting his father up north. Nat excitedly looked forward to his return tomorrow.

In short order, Nat encountered the rocky outcropping. He hoped to find something interesting in the tide pool he could collect, take home, and study. He had learned better than to take a small crab or some other shallow water crustacean or mollusk, because they could not survive the starved environment of his sample container. He was more interested in finding things the ocean returned to shore after being accidentally dropped into the sea. For instance, he liked the way the sea could polish and soften the edges of broken glass or weather a piece of metal. Although most of the time, Nat found only rounded pieces of wood or rusted bottle caps, the hunt was always on for interesting treasure.

Sitting on a rock at the edge of the tide pool, Nat untied his shoes from around his waist and put them on. As his sand-covered ankles met the canvas of his shoes, he wished he had taken the time to rinse his feet. He stood and sure-footedly crossed the rocks, away from the splash zone, until he was up against the eroding face of the bluff. Light, salty foam rimmed the edge of the pockets of water closest to the water line. Where he stood, the water puddles were clear and shallow.

Hoping to find something caught within the rim of one of the small craters, Nat knelt and inspected the dimpled surface of the rocks. A surprised shore crab sidestepped behind a clump of mussels nestled into the crease between the tightly stacked rocks. Camouflaged in greenish-brown patina, a round, brassy disk caught his eye. He picked it up, brought it to eye level, and curiously inspected the evenly shaped hole in its center.

At first inspection, Nat was excited to have found some sort of foreign currency. With coin-like features, the old-looking artifact was about the same size, thickness, and weight of a silver dollar. Possibly portraying some value or purpose, low-relief designs decorated both sides of the medallion. Descriptive markings on both sides were more mysterious than foreign-looking. The symmetrically shaped crescent hole in the center was the tarnished coin's most interesting feature.

Holding the mysterious medallion up to his eye, Nat peered through the crescent opening. As if looking through a spyglass, he surveyed the furthest edge of the tide pool. Nestled between two large rocks just above the water line, the brightly colored corner of a box-like object caught his eye. Pocketing the discolored medallion, Nat moved carefully toward the forward outer edge of the outcropping. As he approached the bright orange object, he could see that it wasn't a box at all, but rather, a mysteriously beautiful case.

Different than anything he had ever before seen, the richly ornate case was covered in a distinctly decorative, thin woven fabric. It had metal, beautifully-sculpted corner edge guards, slightly tarnished, but not the worse for wear. The lavishly-patterned bright fabric, on what looked to be the lid, contained a boldly colorful whimsical mark and several unusual ciphers or letters.

Nat pulled the case free and cautiously looked around – not out of guilt, but out of wanting to do the right thing. Maybe the rightful owner was nearby and he could immediately return it. Making a full turn, Nat looked up the bluff, out to sea, and up and down the shore. Far in the distance behind him, a couple holding hands was leisurely walking away from him. With no clues to go on, Nat sat down and further inspected the elegant package.

The case's size was compact and easily fit on Nat's lap. The finely woven fabric was wet but not stained. The stylish, prominent mark woven in the center of the lid had features that reminded Nat of a compass. Directional coordinates emanated from a spiraled snake centered in rich pastel colors and a golden decorative border. A pair of intricately designed metal latches, on the opposite side of recessed hinges, tightly secured the case. The crisscrossed arms of each latch were inserted into ornate metal plates on the bottom half of the case. No buttons, levers, or keyholes gave a clue as to how the latches released.

Nat had never found anything this remarkable. The magical-looking case was obviously from far away, and possibly from a time long since past. Nat sat frozen, awestruck and uncertain about next steps. He was certain that the intricately crafted case had a meaningful purpose, and possibly held a wonderful treasure or stored a significant secret.

Awkwardly, he slid the case under his t-shirt and nestled it under his left arm. He stood and, while trying to act unaffected and disinterested, made his way back down the beach. Re-encountering the old tire, Nat hesitated at the bottom of the stairs. With the case clutched tightly under his arm, he would have to leave the tire until he had both hands free. Nat carried the case up the stairs, through the back door and into his bedroom, and continued his inspection.

During the walk home, the fabric covering had dried completely. Nat solemnly brushed the surface of the case clean with his hand, stopped, and then slowly felt the surface again. Through the thin decorative fabric at the edges of the whimsical logo, just below the tail of the snake, he felt two raised circular designs. He carefully tried to decipher with his fingers what the raised forms represented. Considering that the images might be as foreign and unusual as those woven into the fabric, he knew he would need to see them – not just feel them.

Nat stood and crossed the room to his desk. Looking through the top drawer, he found his sketchpad and some pencils. Maybe he could use the drawing paper and a soft pencil to make a tracing of the embossed shapes. Mateo and he had once used the technique to make rubbings of old fossils at a Boy Scout meeting. He tore a piece of tissue paper free from the pad and used the side of his pencil tip to rub across the raised shapes. The rubbing revealed a pair of round coin-looking designs, uniform in size, with crescent holes in their centers.

"Nat, are you back there?" called Nat's mother from across the house. Leaving the rubbing on top of his desk, he slid the case under his bed.

"Yeah, Mom. Be right there." Feeling uneasy and secretive, Nat greeted his mother in the kitchen. She reminded him of the chores that needed to be done, especially the agreement they had that he would help her construct her new raised flower box. Several hours later, they admired their accomplishment. Pre-cut, redwood planks had been attached to four short corner posts. Shallow holes were dug at each corner and the frame leveled, side-to-side and diagonally, along the ground. Finally, the shallow wooden box was filed with a blend of garden soil and mulch.

"Thanks for the help, Nat. It looks great and I wouldn't have been able to do it without you. Now I can plant winter vegetables in the fall. Maybe you would like to help me?"

"Sure, Mom," responded Nat authentically.

Dad would soon be home, and Mom reminded Nat that they were all going out to dinner. Nat contentedly drew a deep breath, looked out over the fence, and admired the jewels of bright warm light dancing on the surface of the water. Sitting a few inches above the hazy horizon, the sun ignited the edges of the late-afternoon clouds. A couple of small floating silhouettes moved north toward the small marina in the next town up the coast. Suddenly remembering the case and tracing, Nat shot a look back over his shoulder. The rising moon was still well below the horizon. Heading to the back door, he fingered the weathered medallion in his pocket, feeling for the hole in its center.

Nat rushed to his room and laid the circular medallion over his rubbing from the case. It not only mimicked perfectly the crescent hole in center of the drawings, but was also the same exact size. Between handfuls of garden-soiled t-shirt, Nat polished both surfaces of the coin. He was only slightly surprised when both sides exactly portrayed the designs on his rubbing. Flipping the coin in his hand, he stood locked between unnerving disbelief and hopeful excitement.

Enjoying dinner with his parents, Nat struggled with his decision to keep the mystical case a secret. He rationalized that his parents didn't yet need to be bothered, at least not until he knew more and better understood the coincidence associated with finding the beautiful, locked case and a matching golden locket.

"Does Mateo still get home tomorrow?" asked Nat's dad. Trying to avoid a larger discussion, Nat continued chewing and just nodded seemingly uninterested. "What are your plans for the rest of the summer?" asked Dad, undeterred. School would resume in less than two weeks but, with such a big discovery, Nat could only pretend to know what he would do with the last days of his summer.

"Nothing much. Probably start shooting some hoops. Maybe we will do some treasure hunting on the beach," Nat responded, smiling broadly. The cryptic honesty allowed Nat to feel a little better about his secret.

$\mathcal{A}$s scheduled, Mateo arrived home the following morning. Following breakfast, he found Nat already outside, sitting on the back steps, thinking. After a warm greeting, Nat walked Mateo through the back door and into his bedroom. "You will never guess what I found," he said almost reverently. He casually walked over to the case, picked it up, and placed it in Mateo's lap.

Wide-eyed, Mateo held the case in his outstretched hands and stammered, "Wow! Where did you get this?" After a precise and lively review of the previous day's events, the two of them reviewed Nat's findings.

Mateo inspected the now fully polished, antique-looking medallion and compared it against the tissue rubbing. He picked up a pencil and began to tightly outline the soft, half-tone shapes on the tissue. He referenced both sides of the coin to complete any broken or unclear portions of the tracing. "They're an exact match," he announced confidently.

On one side of the coin, there was a decorative plant motif with a budding flower spiraled around the crescent center hole. The circular outer edge was divided into eight sections by arrows pointing outward, each section divided again by small hash marks – the whole reminding them of the dials on their combination locks at school. On the flip side of the coin, the outer edge was identical in design and alignment. However, the budding flower was replaced with something much more sinister. The crescent hole was now in the center of an ominous, foreboding skull pattern.

With only the mysterious coin in Nat's pocket, the two boys descended the stairs to the beach. They were determined to inspect the tide pool further, hopeful of finding additional medallions or some other remarkable novelty associated with Nat's previous day's bounty. Leaving their shoes on, they sprinted along the wet sand, most of the distance to the shallow pools.

Although the surf was higher this morning, wave sets were still small, and splashed only over the front edge of the rocky shelf. Without hesitation, Nat brought Mateo to the exact spot where the medallion had been discovered. He stood, raised his right hand, with his thumb and forefinger overlapped to form a sight line, and acted out the impossible coincidence of also finding the case.

Together the boys searched every accessible large and small indentation in the tide pool – first generally, and then with precision. Twice they canvassed the cratered surface of the rocks. Failing to find anything in the shallow pools, they meticulously filtered through their fingers the sand on both sides of the rocky bench. Disappointingly, no additional treasure or items associated with the case were found.

The walk home gave Nat and Mateo a chance to discuss what they knew, and consider next steps. The beautifully crafted case held a hidden reference to the medallion. They were found on the same day, a short distance apart, in possibly the liveliest area of the shoreline. Thinking out loud, Nat asked rhetorically, "Was it just good luck that I found both items together?" A few steps later, he added, "They obviously belong together…and the repeating moon design must mean something."

Trying to be helpful, Mateo offered, "Maybe our parents could help us figure this out. They might even know where the case came from." As soon as he said it, he wished he could pull it back. They both instinctively knew that this was their adventure to solve alone.

Sitting on the edge of Nat's bed, Mateo inspected the clasps on the case. With the medallion in his hand, Nat sat down next to him. Each clasp was meticulously crafted out of the same shiny metal as the corner and side guards. Braided tree branches uncurled from the top of the clasp and crisscrossed near the centerline. The silver branches met in a bundle of teardrop leaves and attached to a decorative plate on the bottom half of the case.

Each clasp was secured tightly and showed no signs of play or movement, even when pried with the metal ruler from Nat's desk. In the raised center of each exquisite clasp, between the crossing branches, appeared the raised, recurring shadowed moon – the waxing crescent moon on the left clasp and the opposite waning moon on the right. Nat flipped the medallion in his hand and compared the hole, from both sides, to the raised shapes on the clasps.

With the skull pattern side up, he carefully laid the medallion over the left clasp and effortlessly slid the center hole into place. He flipped the medallion over, flower side up, and anchored it over the right clasp. Nat carefully rotated the medallion counterclockwise a half turn, and the right latch popped lightly free. Nat froze and tossed a wide-eyed look at Mateo. He flipped the medallion over, placed it over the left clasp, and turned it now clockwise with the same result. The boys barely restrained their tandem shout of jubilation. Now sitting as close together as possible, they centered the case across their laps and slowly raised the lid.

The inside of the case was even more spectacular than the outside. Polished amber-colored wood lined the full interior of the case. Inlaid decorative patterns of lighter and darker wood created distinctive borders around the outer edge of both the lid and the bottom. The glossy wood surface showed no imperfections from either withstanding nature's elements or the wear and tear of age. An ingenious weather seal, consisting of two parallel channels in the base and aligned ridges in the lid, appeared to have worked perfectly to keep the sea out.

Inset in two uniform cavities, in the center of the open case, sat two handsomely tooled wooden boxes, each prominently portraying, in raised carvings, opposite sides of the medallion. Nat reached in and, without pulling the box free, opened the lid of the carved flower-blossom box. More than a dozen beautifully clear stones half filled the box. Each stone was perfectly round in diameter and had a domed surface – thinnest at the outer edges. A carved, faceted pattern of stepped diamond shapes decorated the top surface and gave it a jewel-like appearance. Without speaking, both boys picked up a clear stone apiece, and admired the beautiful way it reflected light.

Somewhat unnerved by the evil-looking design of the second handsomely carved box, Mateo reached down and slowly opened the lid with the carved skull motif. Again they found inside beautiful stones, square and black, half filling the box. The uniformly stepped outer edges of the black stones climbed to the center, creating a four-sided pyramid. The black stones were highly polished, completely opaque, and heavier than the clear stones. Holding one of each stone in opposite hands, the boys both figuratively and literally weighed their good fortune.

Immersed in the secrets of the case, both boys jumped at hearing the phone ring on the nightstand next to Nat's bed. Mateo's mom was on the phone and asked that he come home immediately. She had met their new neighbors a few days earlier and wanted Mateo to deliver a plate of freshly baked cookies. The boys were only slightly bothered by the interruption. They knew they would have time later to further explore the stones. It was decided that the case and its contents warranted continued secrecy and that each of them would take, for safekeeping, one clear and one black stone. They closed both carved wooden boxes, and carefully closed the lid on the case. Unaided, the braided metal clasps magically pivoted forward together and securely locked the case with a distinctive, simultaneous click.

With both stones in his pocket, Mateo mounted his bike for the short ride home. The air outside had cooled slightly, but the bright afternoon sun continued to hold the fog far off shore. Brief directions from his mom sent him by foot on his way down their street. Rewarded in advance with his share of warm chocolate chip cookies, Mateo politely introduced himself while offering the housewarming treats. Feeling as if he had done a good job, and proud of his mother's good intentions, Mateo returned home, reported in, and went straight to his room.

He sat down at his desk and turned on his computer. Haunted by the striking marks and decoration of the mystical case, he felt there was more to learn and discover. The bold graphic mark on the lid appeared to reference astrological events, most likely the night sky. The repeating theme of a crescent moon surely was symbolic of some important feature associated with the case and its contents. He wished he had made a sketch to reference.

Mateo began his search by typing "phases of the moon" into his Internet browser. Dozens of websites offered insight into his broad search. After a few sample click-throughs, he found what he was looking for: a lunar calendar diagram. He studied the information on the computer screen and then sent what he had found to his printer.

The full day of exploration and discovery had left Mateo surprisingly fatigued. In preparation for a warm shower, he walked into his closet, took off his shirt, and placed it in the hamper. Realizing he still had the carved stones in his pocket, he pulled them out and opened his hand. The black pyramid-shaped stone rested off-center on top of the clear stone, which was now glowing – giving off white light, as if it were lit from within. Sliding the black stone to the side, Mateo stood spell-bound as the clear stone illuminated the entire closet.

Quickly retrieving his shirt from the hamper and pulling it back on, he raced from the closet. He grabbed his lunar calendar printouts, sprinted out the back door, and pedaled his bike as fast as he could back to Nat's house.

"Look what it does!" Mateo exclaimed, showing off the clear crystal in his cupped hand.

"How did you get it to do that?" asked Nat, reaching for the stone.

"I was in my closet getting undressed, and it was just glowing. Do you think it's getting ready to do something?"

Nat closely inspected the stone. "I hope not something bad," he said pensively, and then carried it into his closet and pulled the door closed, behind closely following Mateo. The stone cast cool brilliant light, completely filling the small space, reaching all four walls and eliminating all shadows.

With more questions than answers, the boys stumbled through the unlatched closet door. Mateo retrieved his research and spread the lunar calendar graph on Nat's desk. He pointed out where the moon was currently in its orbit around the earth – first quarter, and growing to a full moon in less than a week. He did his best to explain his newly acquired insight that the moon completed one full phase from new moon to full moon and back to new moon in thirty days.

The boys compared Mateo's research with the markings on the case. After some study and trial and error, they were confident they had decoded the spiraling logo. They concluded the decorative mark was indeed a lunar calendar of sorts, with each symbol along the spiraling snake representing a phase of the night sky moon's shifting shape. Deciphering the graphic marks in the logo, Mateo pointed to the position on the spiral that indicated the current, almost-fully-lit phase of the moon.

Following the approval of their mothers, Mateo spent the night in a sleeping bag on a foam mat in Nat's room. The time together would provide an opportunity to consider the research Mateo had done online, and to further consider the mysterious stones. By late evening, Mateo's faceted clear stone was no longer luminous. Slowly at first, and then more quickly, the light emanating from the stone appeared to retreat back within the transparent crystal. At the end, a bright spark of light was completely centered inside the stone and hung there, hesitating, just before going out in a moment.

Having fallen asleep later than normal, the boys slept longer than usual. Rejuvenated by a good night's sleep, Mateo held the case in his lap while Nat optimistically once again slid the medallion into place on the left clasp and tried to turn it. When nothing happened, he tried the right clasp, with the same disappointing result. The boys had hoped to more closely inspect the interior of the case, but there had been something distinctively durable and final about the sound the clasps had made the day before when, in unison, they had reattached.

Still confused, but feeling endowed with a new sense of adventure and with treasure in their pockets, Nat and Mateo headed for the bluff and the wooden stairs. Bounding off the bottom step, Nat saw, up against the ice plant, the tread-worn tire, and acknowledged the unfinished task of getting it up the stairs. Once again, they were drawn north up the beach toward the recently fruitful tide pool.

Halfway there, they unhappily encountered a group of boys from school, whom they knew only vaguely by reputation. With just over a week left in their summer vacation, the buddies didn't need an early start with trouble. Playful pranks sometimes eroded to outright bullying, and Nat hoped this was not going to be one of those times. He was several inches taller than Mateo and often fared better in their schoolground coming-of-age hierarchy.

With some bravado in their step, the three slightly older boys purposefully approached the would-be brothers. "How about a contribution?" asked the widest fellow. "We were hoping you would like to help us out with some spare change," he continued with his head cocked to the side disdainfully. "How about it? Just somethin' to help us buy sodas at the harbor."

Both Nat and Mateo had only their stones in their pockets, and they were determined to keep them a secret. "Sorry, we've got nothing for you," responded Nat, trying his best to sound confident.

"No need for trouble, but how about we just look for ourselves?" said the largest boy as he grabbed Mateo, who quickly became the focus of all three ruffians. Nat hesitated only briefly, and then jumped into the fray.

Within seconds, all was settled. Nat wrestled Mateo free from the older boys, dodged a punch aimed at his upper torso, and then stood his ground between both sides. Angered by the roughhousing, Mateo shoved Nat out of his way. "What gives you the right?" he roared, stepped forward, and surprisingly threw his closed fist into the stomach of the boy closest to him. Although the punch didn't carry much force, it was enough to knock the wind out of the would-be thief, and also the fight out of his bullying companions. Mateo continued to throw wild punches, catching only air, until Nat wrapped his arms around him and ended the scuffle.

Defeated in their pride more than their strength, the older boys retreated with a vocal assault on Mateo's sanity. "You should keep him in a cage!" "Yeah, this beach has a leash law!" "How long has he been out of the nuthouse?" The last insult was barely audible over the sound of the breaking waves.

Nat and Mateo sat down in the sand and collected their wits. They were not hurt but, given the close-quarter brawling and shoving, they were understandably agitated. Starting to calm, Mateo felt a sting, a burning high up against his thigh. Both boys reached into their pockets. Mateo produced his stones first and almost dropped them. The black stone glowed red from its center core and was too hot to hold. He juggled the stones between his cupped hands and finally dropped them into the folds of his shirt. Nat looked down at the stones in his hand. Looking at his friend, Mateo acknowledged the bright light illuminating Nat's hand and face.

Once again, within a few hours, both stones returned to normal. It would seem that their stones responded to their actions, possibly bringing attention to their judgment and character. "Do you think they can read our minds?" questioned Mateo aloud.

"They seem to know what we're doing, but I don't know about thoughts," responded Nat. "I wonder if they have any other powers or secrets?" he continued.

$\mathcal{H}$oping to discover the connection between the case and the lunar calendar, the boys decided to inspect the case under the night sky. The boys ate dinner at Mateo's house and then walked together back to Nat's home. The evening was still warm and the night sky clear. While Mateo remained outside, Nat collected the case and medallion from under his bed. Once reunited outside, the boys walked across the moonlit backyard, passing the newly installed garden box, to the furthest corner away from the house. Nat placed the case on the table of their weathered wooden patio furniture. The boys took seats on the same wooden bench on one side of the table.

"What's the plan? asked Mateo. Looking up at the majestic, nearly full moon and then down at the spiraled logo on the case, Nat answered, "I wish I knew. Maybe we will see something under moonlight that we've missed in the past." For several minutes they sat there quietly studying the surface of the case, making eye contact only long enough to recognize neither had a suggestion. Once again without success, Nat placed the medallion on the latches and tried to unlock them.

He pried at the crisscrossed latches with his fingers. Flipping the medallion over in his hand, he felt the embossed areas under the fabric. Almost in desperation, he reached into his pocket, retrieved his stones, and placed one directly over each embossed, circular area.

Almost instantly the case seemed to come alive! Narrow slivers of bright white light began to peek out from the center of the case. As if propelled by the slivers of light, the colorful center logo began to lift off the case, its golden border and bright-colored sections becoming dimensional and several inches tall. The spiraled, spiked snake also took shape, rising up several feet above the case. Its wavy form had the appearance of shiny, colored glass but moved smoothly and naturally. Bold streaks of white light emanated from the tips of several spike-like protrusions along its curved, standing body. The enchanted snake curiously turned its head from side to side, looking at each boy through glowing, bright-red eyes.

Profoundly mesmerized by the beautiful yet ominous reptile, neither boy said a word. Once the snake acknowledged the presence of the boys, it turned its attention downward and stared fiercely at the two stones resting below it on the surface of the case. As if in response to the purposeful stare of the snake, Nat's clear stone began to glow brightly – more dazzling than they had yet seen. Turning its attention toward the dark pyramid-shaped stone, the beautiful serpent regarded it briefly and uncurling, reached down and swallowed it in one quick bite. Recoiling to an upright position, the snake stared knowingly at Nat for several seconds. Finally, it slowly sank back down into the collapsing, beautifully colored base and once again became an inanimate, flat decoration embedded in the logo in the moonlit fabric of the case.

For several seconds the boys sat in silence. They tentatively looked around into the darkness for any unexpected spectators.

Guardian of the Stones

Nat and Mateo Discover the Two Forces of Magic Stones
by Martin Welling

Format: 8 x 10 color casebound

ISBN: 978-1-4327-7692-3

Cover Price: $29.95

Pages: 44

Category: JUVENILE FICTION / Action & Adventure / General

Available at: www.outskirtspress.com/guardianofthestones

Distributed via: Ingram, Baker & Taylor

Published by: Outskirts Press, Inc.

Receive up to 50% off at: www.outskirtspress.com/bookstore

Publication Date: Feb 10, 2012

Nat and Mateo are best friends. They enjoy all the beautiful things their home has to offer… the sun, the beach, the ocean, and all the adventure they can find along the shoreline. But one day, the sea brings forth a gift the boys don't expect… a beautiful and mysterious carved box, which holds secrets inside it that will seal the boys' friendship for a lifetime, and which will teach them more about who they truly are. This beautifully written modern fable, full of discovery and enchantment, is a delight for readers of all ages.

creative analytical problem-solving and creative design aesthetics. He has spent over two decades in progressively challenging creative roles; for the past ten years he has been a senior executive, working as a department head overseeing licensed product development in the sports and entertainment industry. This is his second book dedicated to his three grandchildren.

For more information, visit http://outskirtspress.com/guardianofthestones

Outskirts Press, Inc., 10940 S. Parker Rd - 515, Parker CO 80134 Phone: 888-672-6657 Fax: 888-208-8601

Nat finally reached over and retrieved his still-glowing clear stone from off the case. "I wasn't expecting that!" he whispered excitedly. Examining the clear stone in his open hand, he said, "I think it's a little larger and heavier than it was before."

Mateo reached into his pocket and produced his stones for comparison. "Here! Compare it to mine." Nat's clear stone had not only grown larger, but it now had a small, black pyramid in its center. It was as if his two stones had become one.

Confident that they were still alone, and hoping for a repeat of the miraculous last few minutes, Mateo excitedly placed his stones on the case. Once again the lustrous serpent materialized from the flat, two-dimensional logo, heroically rose up in an apron of spiked light, and stared insightfully at Mateo. Repeating its earlier actions, the serpent regarded the stones on the case, prompted a miraculous, illuminating response, and then swallowed the black stone in one quick motion.

Unbeknownst to Nat and Mateo, the events of this night were an initiation for the two of them. For the next thirty days, one full cycle of the moon around the earth, their enchanted stones reacted to their thoughts, words, and actions. When they went out of their way to help others, to provide encouragement, to tell the truth, the stones gave off the purest light and even lit their way in the dark when necessary. When they ignored those in need around them, when they lost their temper, shaded the truth, or were disrespectful, the black pyramid glowed as if ready to melt the clear stone. One evening, after telling his father he wasn't feeling well to avoid helping with the chores after dinner, Nat's stone glowed so hotly that it left a permanent circular scorch mark on his desk.

With the start of school, Nat and Mateo were engaged in a competition of sorts, seeing how often they could produce light with their stones. Daily, they recorded their progress on calendars they made, adorned with their drawings of the case's lunar calendar logo. A circle was drawn on the days their stones glowed, and a pyramid on the infrequent days they felt burning heat. Some uncommon days included both marks. To avoid drawing unwanted attention, they made it a practice to carry their stones in black pouches, made from repurposed materials found in Mateo's garage.

Nat was dreaming deeply and awoke disoriented and confused when prodded by his mother. It was Monday morning, the beginning of the second week of school. Although he didn't mind going to school, he hadn't yet gotten used to getting up on a schedule. "Time to get up, Nat, or you are going to be late," encouraged his mother as she opened the shades. Clumsily he rolled out of bed, ending up on all fours on the floor. He tossed a glance at the beautiful, mysterious case stored under his bed. He couldn't help wondering if it still held secrets that needed to be discovered?

Following their normal practice, Nat and Mateo met on the corner for their short bike ride to school. They had ended up in different classes this year, but both liked their teachers and they were lucky to have the same daily schedule. The secrets and insights they shared made them even better friends, and each trusted the other completely.

Shortly after lunch, Nat was working through his fifth period history exam. He was prepared and felt confident he knew the answers to most, if not all, of the Civil War facts they were being quizzed on. A few of the students around him had already finished. He accidentally made eye contact with Sarah a couple of rows over. She smiled and he felt himself begin to blush. Sarah was smart and pretty, and he had secretly hoped they would be in the same class this year. He quickly looked down at the final few questions when, without warning, everything seemed to come apart.

Two hard jolts shook the room, throwing several students off balance and almost out of their seats. The jolts were replaced by a continuously rolling, shaking motion that quickly sent the contents and occupants of the room into chaos. The long row of windows facing the inner courtyard shattered almost in complete unison, the shards of glass raining down on to the floor. As shocked and screaming students scrambled to safety below their desks, ceiling tiles fell with large thuds. Some pulled light fixtures down with them, burying the length of the room in several inches of debris.

In a few seconds, the shaking slowed and the ground movement stopped. When it seemed that the worst might be over, Nat turned toward the heavy, thick, cracking noise coming from the other side of the classroom. From under his desk, he watched the long, tall brick wall wobble and a large crack sever it halfway along its length. Nat watched in disbelief as half the wall collapsed sideways, completely burying several rows of student desks in heavy rubble.

Thick dust filled the room, limiting visibility to almost zero. Nat freed himself from some light wreckage and quickly climbed out from under his desk. In the grit-induced twilight, he could discern that he was the only student unhampered and standing. He surveyed the destruction around him and immediately recognized the most pressing need to free the students from below the collapsed wall. He quickly but carefully crossed the room and stood at the edge of the fallen heavy concrete section.

Still struggling to see clearly in the darkened room, he reached into his pocket and retrieved his black pouch. Pulling the drawstrings open, he barely noticed the stone already glowing. He pulled the stone free and held it in his outstretched hand. Light filled the space around him, making the earthquake's destruction all the more distinguishable. In a slow spiraling motion, the glowing crystal amazingly floated off Nat's hand and hung in the air directly above the collapsed wall.

Spiraling with increasing speed, the clear stone glowed the purest and brightest light Nat had yet witnessed. Bold spikes of twirling light emanated from its center and pierced the collapsed section of wall. Silently building to a blurred, spherical crescendo, the stone seemed to hang motionless for a second, and then flashed a blinding burst of white light.

The next thing Nat knew, he was sitting on the ground. The dust within the room was settling and visibility had improved. The large collapsed section of wall was gone. Small fragments of masonry covered several rows of the bent and dented desks in front of him. Covered in grey dust, several students were climbing out from under their desks and beginning to stand. All at once, the room was alive with the noise of young voices responding to the arriving emergency personnel. Looking down, Nat did a quick assessment of his own condition and opened his right closed fist. Shaking his head and smiling, he closed his hand tightly around the dazzling, beautiful stone.

Nat slowly climbed to his feet. A well-equipped fireman was gathering his dust-covered classmates together and leading them out the door to the inner courtyard. Nat recognized Sarah at the back of the line and hustled to get in line behind her. "Are you ok?" he asked with more than usual concern. The question was wholly inadequate but it was the best he could do. Sarah could only nod her head, and said nothing.

Surveying the line of students in front of him, Nat could see the others, like Sarah, were frightened but unharmed. Once outside, a thorough accounting of the students provided the best news – but for a few cuts and bruises, everyone was safe and accounted for.

About a half hour later, Nat found Mateo huddled with the rest of his class outside their classroom. A muscular paramedic was applying dressings to students who had suffered a few minor scrapes and cuts. Parents had begun to arrive, adding a renewed level of chaos and anxiety. Nat had been unreasonably confident that his best friend had not been harmed. He was relieved to see that his intuition had been correct. Seemingly acknowledging the miraculous events that had taken place, Mateo smiled broadly as Nat approached and met his gaze.

All the students were directed to the sports fields, away from the damaged classrooms. As their moms chatted excitedly, Nat and Mateo shared their individual heroic stories. "It freed them!" Nat began as he proudly told of the stone's miraculous power. "The wall just collapsed. I knew I had to do something and it was as if the stone knew what I was thinking. It floated in the air and spun around so fast," he voice trailing off, "and then it happened."

Matching Nat's instinct and experience during the dangerous turbulence, Mateo had also pulled his transparent stone out of his pocket and, from under his desk, held it in his outstretched, open hand. As things seemed at their darkest and most perilous, Mateo's stone filled the space above him with a light so pure and bright that it seemed to protect all the students from falling debris and thus serious injury. Amazingly, in the chaos and limited visibility of both rooms, no students seemed to have witnessed the miraculous safeguard provided by the boys' stones.

Over the next few days, it became clear that two safest places to be at the school during the earthquake had been in Nat and Mateo's classrooms. Although most of the school's buildings had sustained less damage then the boys had withstood, several student injuries required specialized treatment and hospitalization. Thankfully, it was expected that none of the injuries would require long recoveries.

*F*or the next week, as debris was cleared around their school and temporary classrooms delivered, Nat and Mateo spent as much time together as possible. They had watched the moon complete its last quarter and charted its progress toward a completely dark new moon. Encouraged by their newfound power and feeling somewhat invincible, they began to see themselves as uniquely important and special. Proudly a few times, they discussed how they might engage the stones in more self-serving ways. Each time their blossoming arrogance entered their conversations, they could feel their stones searing in their pockets. So immediate were the stones' skin-burning reactions to their prideful thoughts, that the boys knew they needed to temper their hubris. Although the stones were in their possession, it became obvious that they could not or would not be used to further their personal ambitions.

The fourth week began with the reopening of the school in temporary trailers. Following the week off, Nat looked forward to seeing his classmates again, especially Sarah. The trailers looked new and, although smaller than their brick and mortar predecessors, they were furnished with modern, fashionable desks and the latest computers. Following the confusion associated with finding their right classrooms, Nat, Mateo and the rest of students settled into their new accommodations. An outdoor assembly had been scheduled just prior to lunch at

the newly installed sports field bleachers. The city mayor welcomed the students back and provided encouragement. As the fire captain acknowledged the bravery of all the students and staff during the disaster, Nat and Mateo modestly, almost imperceptibly, nudged each other with their clenched fists.

For almost a month, the moon had progressed from fully illuminated and bright to fully in shadow and dark, and back to a majestic full moon. Similarly Nat and Mateo had grown through a progression of discovery and uncertainty, through a short stint of smugness, and on to courage and understanding. One full cycle through the phases of the moon had opened their eyes to the impact they had on those around them, especially their friends and family. Their stones had grown in size, but more importantly, their perceptions and understanding of their place in the world had matured and blossomed.

Thirty days from the time they were christened by the mystical viper, the stones no longer produced their effects. Larger acts of kindness and greater sensitivity did not coax the stones back to life. For twenty-nine days, the stones had been their moral compasses of sorts, enhancing their self-awareness and strengthening the bond between them. Their unlighted stillness weighed heavily on the Nat and Mateo alike.

After repeated tries, the boys gave up trying to reopen the case. Twice to no avail, under moonlit nights, they strategically placed their stones on the case. Unfortunately, it seemed their miraculous prize had an expiration date that couldn't be renewed. With their limited draftsman skills, Nat and Mateo spent a few weeks making detailed drawings of the case and the clasps. Now in plain view, the boys' cherished stones rested in prominent locations in their individual bedrooms. Every night before falling asleep, Nat would glance over at the gemstone on his desk, hoping to see even the faintest glow.

After a few months, Nat was confident he needed to do something with the beautiful case and its bounty of charmed crystals. Believing that finding the case was not coincidental, he was certain that he needed to effectively pass it on. Late one afternoon, with the case under his t-shirt and under his arm, he met Mateo at his back door. "I think it's time. Are you ready for this?"

Mateo answered frankly, "No, I'm not. I don't see why you won't let it be. You should just the keep the case."

"Come on, Mateo, it's been weeks and the case has never again opened for us," argued Nat steadfastly. In silence, they bounded down the thirty steps to the beach and quietly walked north. Too quickly, they arrived at the tide pool and climbed onto the rocks.

Carefully standing together on the outer raised wet edge against the surf, Nat brushed the beautiful surface of the case with his hand. He ran his finger over the ornate corner guards and tested the security of the intricate claps. It was just a beautiful relic, but its contents and mystical surprises had made it a wonderfully rich prize. Looking out at the horizon, Nat stood motionless for several minutes, and then knowingly held eye contact with Mateo. Trying not to hold anything back, he held the case in both hands, wound at the waist, and with a full, unwinding extension of his upper torso, tossed the case into the sea.

Repealing the onslaught of the breaking waves, the buoyant, bright orange case quickly moved out and away from the tide pool. In a straight line, it moved through the foamy surf and up and over the last set of forming waves. Once free from the pull of the tide along the shoreline, the case appeared to move more quickly away from the shoreline and then came to a stop.

Lingering briefly, the enchanted case sprang to life! Repeating the splendor of his earlier visit, the resident enchanted reptile rose from the top of the case. It stood much taller than before – several feet tall with spikes of beautiful light emanating from its sides and shooting out across the water. The serpent appeared to recognize the boys standing on the rocks, and held their gaze. Nat looked into its transparent red eyes and felt a profound connection. For a moment, time stood still and then, as if weighted down by the wise-looking serpent, the case began to sink below the surface of the sun-washed afternoon sea. Partially submerged, the snake began to shrink and retreat back into the case, bold streaks of light brightly illuminating the sea in all directions.

*O*ver time, Nat began to wear the polished crescent-pierced coin, threaded by a leather string, around his neck. He was confident there were more medallions out there, and this one was his to keep and treasure. Possibly someday, he would encounter someone who held a match, or he would come across another mystical treasure connected to it. It had led him to the beautiful, ageless case and the magical stones – but more importantly, it had led Mateo and him to their best selves.

Outside their normal routine, Mateo met Nat at the back door. Running a little late, they jumped on their bikes for their short trip to school. Without thinking, Nat reached down, grasped the medallion hanging around his neck, and gently inserted it over his collar and under his shirt. "So what's up with you and Sarah?" taunted Mateo with a broad smile on his face.

"Nothing to talk about and none of your business," responded Nat, hoping the physical exertion would hide the blushing of his cheeks. Shortly, the boys were pedaling hard, locked in a head-to-head race to what would prove to be not only a very good day, but also the beginning of a very bright future.

CPSIA information can be obtained
at www.ICGtesting.com
Printed in the USA
LVIC040127190312
273549LV00001B